STEPHEN KING

THE LIFE OF CHUCK

SCRIBNER

New York Amsterdam/Antwerp London
Toronto Sydney/Melbourne New Delhi

Scribner
An Imprint of Simon & Schuster, LLC
1230 Avenue of the Americas
New York, NY 10020

Copyright © 2020 by Stephen King

This story was previously published in *If It Bleeds*

All rights reserved, including the right to reproduce this book or portions thereof in
any form whatsoever. For information, address Scribner Subsidiary Rights Department,
1230 Avenue of the Americas, New York, NY 10020.

First Scribner hardcover edition June 2025

SCRIBNER and design are trademarks of Simon & Schuster, LLC

Simon & Schuster strongly believes in freedom of expression and stands against
censorship in all its forms. For more information, visit BooksBelong.com.

For information about special discounts for bulk purchases, please contact
Simon & Schuster Special Sales at 1-866-506-1949 or business@simonandschuster.com.

The Simon & Schuster Speakers Bureau can bring authors to your live event.
For more information or to book an event, contact the Simon & Schuster Speakers Bureau
at 1-866-248-3049 or visit our website at www.simonspeakers.com.

Interior design by Kyle Kabel

Manufactured in the United States of America

1   3   5   7   9   10   8   6   4   2

ISBN 978-1-6682-0878-6
ISBN 978-1-6682-0879-3 (ebook)

THE LIFE
OF CHUCK

AN INTRODUCTION

The story should never have existed, at least not in the form it finally took. That it has become a movie—a most *excellent* movie, in my humble opinion—is even more unlikely. And yet, here we are.

Life can be full of nasty surprises, as most of us know, but—as most of us also know—every now and then something good happens. I'm tempted to say, "It's the good things that make all the crap worthwhile," but the jury's still out on that one. All I can do is tell you how this particular good thing happened; it's up to you to figure out the rest. Watching the film, especially the transcendent last few minutes, may help you in that regard.

Stories come when they will; you just have to be open to their arrival. One day on my morning walk, I was musing on an African proverb that says, "When an old man dies, a library burns down." (I might have been thinking about that particular proverb because I'm getting on in years myself.) The proverb led me to think about Walt Whitman's "Song of Myself," where he says, "I am large, I contain multitudes." I thought to myself, *What if it isn't a library that burns when a man dies? What if it's a whole world? His world?*

I liked the idea enough to write a short story called "The Life of Chuck," which was about the entire world—hell, the entire *universe*—slowly going down the tubes because the man who perceived it, one Charles Krantz, was dying of a brain tumor.

That was all. Story done, over and out. I put it in a drawer, thinking I'd rewrite it later on.

Fast-forward a month or so. I'm in Boston for a couple of Red Sox games, staying at the Mandarin Oriental Hotel (which my kids persist in calling the Mandarin Orange). Across the street, outside the drugstore, a young man is beating on a couple of overturned plastic buckets. Your basic busker, in other words, with an upturned hat in front of him for contributions. This time I thought, *What if some random Mr. Businessman stopped and began to jive? And what if he actually began to dance?* Then, a real inspiration, the kind of thing a writer lives for: *And what if that guy was Chuck Krantz, with his brain tumor just beginning to announce itself?*

That was too cool not to write, because it was about the joy of life in the shadow of death. It never occurred to me that there might be a third story, but I did like the way Chuck's life went *backward*, from his death to his final months as a healthy man. I began to play with the idea of a final act (which eventually turned out to be Act 1), with Chuck as a kid, learning to dance and discovering the rather unpleasant secret in his grandpa's cupola. I wanted Chuck to *know* he was going to die. Because, dig it, we all *do* know, don't we? We just kind of pretend the elephant in the room is a big gray sofa.

In the end, I had three loosely connected stories. I had to smooth them out and whittle them a bit here and there to make the fit a little tighter, but they finally came together.

Luckily for me, Mike Flanagan wrote a script that turned the story's funky back-to-front format into a virtue and made it as an indie film at a time when few films were being made due to Covid and multiple strikes by film and television creators. Mike was able to thread the needle on that one because the screenplay was written pre-strike, and the film itself bypassed the major Hollywood studios.

In short, dear reader, it was a miracle that the story got written, a double miracle that such a strange piece of work should become a film, and a triple miracle that the film is such a splendid little gem.

—Stephen King
March 30, 2024

ACT III

THANKS, CHUCK!

The day Marty Anderson saw the billboard was just before the Internet finally went down for good. It had been wobbling for eight months since the first short interruptions. Everyone agreed it was only a matter of time, and everyone agreed they would muddle through somehow once the wired-in world finally went dark— after all, they had managed without it, hadn't they? Besides, there were other problems, like whole species of birds and fish dying off, and now there was California to think about: going, going, possibly soon to be gone.

Marty was late leaving school, because it was that least favorite day for high school educators, the one set aside for parent-teacher conferences. As this one had played out, Marty had found few parents interested in discussing little Johnny and little Janey's progress (or lack of it). Mostly they wanted to discuss the probable final failure of the Internet, which would sink their Facebook and Instagram accounts for good. None of them mentioned Pornhub, but Marty suspected many of the parents who showed up—female as well as male—were mourning that site's impending extinction.

Ordinarily, Marty would have driven home by way of the turnpike bypass, zippity-zip, home in a jiff, but that wasn't possible due to the collapse of the bridge over Otter Creek. That had happened four months ago, and there was no sign of repairs; just orange-striped wooden barriers that already looked dingy and were covered with taggers' logos.

With the bypass closed, Marty was forced to drive directly through downtown to reach his house on Cedar Court along with everybody else who lived on the east side. Thanks to the conferences, he'd left at five instead of three, at the height of rush hour, and a drive that would have taken twenty minutes in the old days would take at least an hour, probably longer because some of the traffic lights were out, as well. It was stop-and-go all the way, with plenty of horns, screeching brakes, bumper-kisses, and waved middle fingers. He was stopped for ten minutes at the intersection of Main and Market, so had plenty of time to notice the billboard on top of the Midwest Trust building.

Until today, it had advertised one of the airlines, Delta or Southwest, Marty couldn't remember which. This afternoon the happy crew of arm-in-arm flight attendants had been replaced by a photograph of a moon-faced man with black-framed glasses that matched his black, neatly combed hair. He was sitting at a desk with a pen in his hand, jacketless but with his tie carefully knotted at the collar of his white shirt. On the hand holding the pen there was a crescent-shaped scar that had for some reason not been airbrushed out. To Marty he looked like an accountant. He was smiling cheerfully down at the snarled twilight traffic from his perch high atop the bank building. Above his head, in blue, was CHARLES KRANTZ. Below his desk, in red, was 39 GREAT YEARS! THANKS, CHUCK!

Marty had never heard of Charles "Chuck" Krantz, but supposed he must have been a pretty big bug at Midwest Trust to rate a retirement photo on a spotlit billboard that had to be at least fifteen feet high and

5

fifty feet across. And the photo must be an old one, if he'd put in almost forty years, or his hair would have been white.

"Or gone," Marty said, and brushed at his own thinning thatch. He took a chance at downtown's main intersection five minutes later, when a momentary hole opened up. He squirted his Prius through it, tensing for a collision and ignoring the shaken fist of a man who squelched to a stop only inches from t-boning him.

There was another tie-up at the top of Main Street, and another close call. By the time he got home he had forgotten all about the billboard. He drove into the garage, pushed the button that lowered the door, and then just sat for a full minute, breathing deeply and trying not to think about having to run the same gauntlet tomorrow morning. With the bypass closed, there was just no other choice. If he wanted to go to work at all, that was, and right then taking a sick day (he had plenty of them stacked up) seemed like a more attractive option.

"I wouldn't be the only one," he told the empty garage. He knew this to be true. According to the

New York Times (which he read on his tablet every morning if the Internet was working), absenteeism was at a worldwide high.

He grabbed his stack of books with one hand and his battered old briefcase with the other. It was heavy with papers that would need correcting. Thus burdened, he struggled out of the car and closed the door with his butt. The sight of his shadow on the wall doing something that looked like a funky dance move made him laugh. The sound startled him; laughter in these difficult days was hard to come by. Then he dropped half of his books on the garage floor, which put an end to any nascent good humor.

He gathered up *Introduction to American Literature* and *Four Short Novels* (he was currently teaching *The Red Badge of Courage* to his sophomores) and went inside. He had barely managed to get everything on the kitchen counter before the phone rang. The landline, of course; there was hardly any cell coverage these days. He sometimes congratulated himself on keeping his landline when so many of his colleagues had given theirs up. Those folks were truly hung,

7

because getting one put in this last year or so . . . forget about it. You'd be more likely to be using the turnpike bypass again before you got to the top of the waiting list, and even the landlines now had frequent outages.

Caller ID no longer worked, but he was sure enough about who was on the other end to simply pick up the phone and say, "Yo, Felicia."

"Where have you been?" his ex-wife asked him. "I've been trying to reach you for an hour!"

Marty explained about the parent-teacher conferences, and the long trip home.

"Are you okay?"

"I will be, as soon as I get something to eat. How are you, Fel?"

"I'm getting along, but we had six more today."

Marty didn't have to ask her six more of what. Felicia was a nurse at City General, where the nursing staff now called itself the Suicide Squad.

"Sorry to hear that."

"Sign of the times." He could hear the shrug in her voice, and thought that two years ago—when they'd still been married—six suicides in one day would have left her shaken, heartbroken, and sleepless. But you could get used to anything, it seemed.

"Are you still taking your ulcer medication, Marty?" Before he could reply, she hurried on. "It's not nagging, just concern. Divorce doesn't mean I still don't care about you, y'know?"

"I know, and I am." This was half a lie, because the doctor-prescribed Carafate was now impossible to get, and he was relying on Prilosec. He told the half-lie because he still cared about her, too. They actually got along better now that they weren't married anymore. There was even sex, and although it was infrequent, it was pretty damn good. "I appreciate you asking."

"Really?"

"Yes, ma'am." He opened the fridge. Pickings were slim, but there were hotdogs, a few eggs, and a can of blueberry yogurt he would save for a pre-bedtime snack. Also three cans of Hamm's.

"Good. How many parents actually showed up?"

"More than I expected, far less than a full house. Mostly they wanted to talk about the Internet. They seemed to think I should know why it keeps shitting

9

the bed. I had to keep telling them I'm an English teacher, not an IT guy."

"You know about California, right?" Lowering her voice, as if imparting a great secret.

"Yes." That morning a gigantic earthquake, the third in the last month and by far the worst, had sent another large chunk of the Golden State into the Pacific Ocean. The good news was that most of that part of the state had been evacuated. The bad news was that now hundreds of thousands of refugees were trekking east, turning Nevada into one of the most populous states in the union. Gasoline in Nevada currently cost twenty bucks a gallon. Cash only, and if the station wasn't tapped out.

Marty grabbed a half-empty quart of milk, sniffed, and drank from the bottle in spite of the faintly suspicious aroma. He needed a real drink, but knew from bitter experience (and sleepless nights) that he had to insulate his stomach first.

He said, "It's interesting to me that the parents who did show up seemed more concerned about the Internet than the California quakes. I suppose because the state's breadbasket regions are still there."

"But for how long? I heard a scientist on NPR say that California is peeling away like old wallpaper. And another Japanese reactor got inundated this afternoon. They're saying it was shut down, all's well, but I don't think I believe that."

"Cynic."

"We're living in cynical times, Marty." She hesitated. "Some people think we're living in the Last Times. Not just the religious crazies, either. Not anymore. You heard that from a member in good standing of the City General Suicide Squad. We lost six today, true, but there were eighteen more we dragged back. Most with the help of Naloxone. But . . ." She lowered her voice again. ". . . supplies of that are getting very thin. I heard the head pharmacist saying we might be completely out by the end of the month."

"That sucks," Marty said, eyeing his briefcase. All those papers waiting to be processed. All those spelling errors waiting to be corrected. All those dangling subordinate clauses and vague conclusions waiting to be red-inked. Computer crutches like Spellcheck and apps like Grammar Alert didn't seem to help. Just thinking of it made him tired. "Listen, Fel, I ought to

11

go. I have tests to grade and essays on 'Mending Wall' to correct." The thought of the stacked vapidities in those waiting essays made him feel old.

"All right," Felicia said. "Just . . . you know, touching base."

"Roger that." Marty opened the cupboard and took down the bourbon. He would wait until she was off the phone to pour it, lest she hear the glugging and know what he was doing. Wives had intuition; ex-wives seemed to develop high-def radar.

"Could I say I love you?" she asked.

"Only if I can say it right back," Marty replied, running his finger over the label on the bottle: Early Times. A very good brand, he thought, for these later times.

"I love you, Marty."

"And I love you."

A good place to end, but she was still there. "Marty?"

"What, hon?"

"The world is going down the drain, and all we can say is 'that sucks.' So maybe we're going down the drain, too."

12

"Maybe we are," he said, "but Chuck Krantz is retiring, so I guess there's a gleam of light in the darkness."

"Thirty-nine great years," she responded, and it was her turn to laugh.

He put the milk down. "You saw the billboard?"

"No, it was an ad on the radio. That NPR show I was telling you about."

"If they're running ads on NPR, it really is the end of the world," Marty said. She laughed again, and the sound made him glad. "Tell me, how does Chuck Krantz rate this kind of coverage? He looks like an accountant, and I never heard of him."

"No idea. The world is full of mysteries. No hard stuff, Marty. I know you're thinking of it. Have a beer, instead."

He didn't laugh as he ended the call, but he smiled. Ex-wife radar. High-def. He put the Early Times back in the cupboard and grabbed a beer instead. He plopped a couple of hotdogs into water and went into his little study to see if the Internet was up while he waited for the water to boil.

It was, and seemed to be running at slightly better

13

than its usual slow crawl. He went to Netflix, thinking he might re-watch an episode of *Breaking Bad* or *The Wire* while he ate his dogs. The welcome screen came up, showing selections that hadn't changed since last evening (and the stuff on Netflix used to change just about every day, not so long ago), but before he could decide on which bad guy he wanted to watch, Walter White or Stringer Bell, the welcome screen disappeared. SEARCHING appeared, and the little worry circle.

"Fuck," Marty said. "Gone for the ni—"

Then the worry circle disappeared and the screen came back. Only it wasn't the Netflix welcome screen; it was Charles Krantz, sitting at his paper-strewn desk, smiling with his pen in his scarred hand. CHARLES KRANTZ above him; 39 GREAT YEARS! THANKS, CHUCK! below.

"Who the fuck are you, Chuckie?" Marty asked. "How do you rate?" And then, as if his breath had blown out the Internet like a birthday candle, the picture disappeared and the words on the screen were CONNECTION LOST.

It did not come back that night. Like half of

California (soon to be three-quarters), the Internet had vanished.

The first thing Marty noticed the next day as he backed his car out of the garage was the sky. How long had it been since he had seen that clear unblemished blue? A month? Six weeks? The clouds and the rain (sometimes a drizzle, sometimes a torrent) were almost constant now, and on days when the clouds cleared, the sky usually remained bleary from the smoke of fires in the Midwest. They had blackened most of Iowa and Nebraska, and were moving on to Kansas, driven by gale-force winds.

The second thing he noticed was Gus Wilfong trudging up the street with his oversized lunchbox banging against his thigh. Gus was wearing khakis, but with a tie. He was a supervisor at the city's public works department. Although it was only quarter past seven, he looked tired and out of sorts, as if at the end of a long day instead of just starting one. And if he was just starting one, why was he walking toward his house next door to Marty's? Also . . .

15

Marty powered down his window. "Where's your car?"

Gus's short laugh was humorless. "Parked on the sidewalk halfway down Main Street Hill, along with about a hundred others." He blew out his breath. "Whoo, I can't remember the last time I walked three miles. Which probably says more about me than you want to know. If you're going to school, buddy, you're going to have to go all the way out Route 11 and then hook back on Route 19. Twenty miles, at least, and there'll be plenty of traffic there, too. You might arrive in time for lunch, but I wouldn't count on it."

"What happened?"

"Sinkhole opened up at the intersection of Main and Market. Man, it's huge. All the rain we've been having might have something to do with it, lack of maintenance probably even more. Not my department, thank God. Got to be twenty cars at the bottom of it, maybe thirty, and some of the people in those cars . . ." He shook his head. "They ain't coming back."

"Jesus," Marty said. "I was just there last evening. Backed up in traffic."

"Be glad you weren't there this morning. Mind if I get in with you? Sit down for a minute? I'm pooped, and Jenny will have gone back to bed. I don't want to wake her up, especially with bad news."

"Sure."

Gus got in the car. "This is bad, my friend."

"It sucks," Marty agreed. It was what he'd said to Felicia last night. "Just got to grin and bear it, I guess."

"I'm not grinning," Gus said.

"Planning to take the day off?"

Gus raised his hands and brought them down on the lunchbox in his lap. "I don't know. Maybe I'll make some calls, see if someone can pick me up, but I'm not hopeful."

"If you do take the day, don't plan to spend it watching Netflix or YouTube videos. Internet's down again, and I've got a feeling it might be for good this time."

"I'm assuming you know about California," Gus said.

"I didn't turn on the TV this morning. Slept in a bit." He paused. "Didn't want to watch it anyway, to tell you the truth. Is there something new?"

17

"Yeah. The rest of it went." He reconsidered. "Well . . . they're saying twenty per cent of northern California is still hanging in there, which means probably ten, but the food-producing regions are gone."

"That's terrible." It was, of course, but instead of horror and terror and grief, all Marty felt was a kind of benumbed dismay.

"You could say that," Gus agreed. "Especially with the Midwest turning to charcoal and the southern half of Florida now basically swampland fit only for alligators. I hope you've got a lot of food in your pantry and freezer, because now *all* the major food-producing regions of this country are gone. The same with Europe. It's already famine-time in Asia. Millions dead there. Bubonic plague, I'm hearing."

They sat in Marty's driveway, watching more people walking back from downtown, many dressed in suits and ties. A woman in a pretty pink suit was trudging along in sneakers, carrying her heels in one hand. Marty thought her name was Andrea something, lived a street or two over. Hadn't Felicia told him she worked at Midwest Trust?

"And the bees," Gus continued. "They were in trouble even ten years ago, but now they're completely gone, except for a few hives down in South America. No more honey, honey. And without them to pollinate whatever crops might be left . . ."

"Excuse me," Marty said. He got out of the car and trotted to catch up with the woman in the pink suit. "Andrea? Are you Andrea?"

She turned warily, lifting her shoes as if she might have to use one of the heels to ward him off. Marty understood; there were plenty of loosely wrapped people around these days. He stopped five feet away. "I'm Felicia Anderson's husband." Ex, actually, but husband sounded less potentially dangerous. "I think you and Fel know each other."

"We do. I was on the Neighborhood Watch Committee with her. What can I do for you, Mr. Anderson? I've had a long walk and my car's stuck in what appears to be a terminal traffic jam downtown. As for the bank, it's . . . leaning."

"Leaning," Marty repeated. In his mind he saw an image of the Leaning Tower of Pisa. With Chuck Krantz's retirement photo on top.

19

"It's on the edge of the sinkhole and although it hasn't fallen in, it looks very unsafe to me. Sure to be condemned. I suppose that's the end of my job, at least in the downtown branch, but I don't really care. I just want to go home and put my feet up."

"I was curious about the billboard on the bank building. Have you seen it?"

"How could I miss it?" she asked. "I work there, after all. I've also seen the graffiti, which is everywhere—we love you Chuck, Chuck lives, Chuck forever—and the ads on TV."

"Really?" Marty thought of what he'd seen on Netflix last night, just before it went away. At the time he'd dismissed it as a particularly annoying pop-up ad.

"Well, the local stations, anyway. Maybe it's different on cable, but we don't get that anymore. Not since July."

"Us, either." Now that he had begun the fiction that he was still part of an us, it seemed best to carry on with it. "Just channel 8 and channel 10."

Andrea nodded. "No more ads for cars or Eliquis or Bob's Discount Furniture. Just Charles Krantz, thirty-nine great years, thanks, Chuck. A full minute of that, then back to our regularly scheduled reruns. Very peculiar, but these days, what isn't? Now I really want to get home."

"This Charles Krantz isn't associated with your bank? *Retiring* from the bank?"

She paused for just a moment before continuing her homeward trudge, carrying high heels she would not need that day. Perhaps ever again. "I don't know Charles Krantz from Adam. He must have worked in the Omaha headquarters. Although from what I understand, Omaha is just a great big ashtray these days."

Marty watched her go. So did Gus Wilfong, who had joined him. Gus nodded at the glum parade of returning workers who could no longer get to their jobs—selling, trading, banking, waiting on tables, making deliveries.

"They look like refugees," Gus said.

"Yeah," Marty said. "They kind of do. Hey, you remember asking me about my food supplies?"

Gus nodded.

"I have quite a few cans of soup. Also some basmati and Rice-A-Roni. Cheerios, I believe. As for the

21

freezer, I think I might have six TV dinners and half a pint of Ben & Jerry's."

"You don't sound concerned."

Marty shrugged. "What good would that do?"

"But see, it's interesting," Gus said. "We were all concerned at first. We wanted answers. People went to Washington and protested. Remember when they knocked over the White House fence and those college kids got shot?"

"Yeah."

"There was the government overthrow in Russia and the Four Day War between India and Pakistan. There's a volcano in Germany, for Christ's sake— *Germany*! We told each other all this would blow over, but that doesn't seem to be happening, does it?"

"No," Marty agreed. Although he'd just gotten up, he felt tired. Very. "Not blowing over, blowing harder."

"Then there's the suicides."

Marty nodded. "Felicia sees them every day."

"I think the suicides will slow down," Gus said, "and people will just wait."

"For what?"

"For the end, pal. The end of everything. We've been going through the five stages of grief, don't you get it? Now we've arrived at the last one. Acceptance."

Marty said nothing. He could think of nothing to say.

"There's so little curiosity now. And all this . . ." Gus waved an arm. "It came out of nowhere. I mean, we knew the environment was going to the dogs—I think even the right-wing nutjobs secretly believed in it—but this is sixty different varieties of shit, all at once." He gave Marty a look that was almost pleading. "In how long? A year? Fourteen months?"

"Yes," Marty said. "Sucks." It seemed to be the only word that fit.

Overhead they heard a droning sound and looked up. The big jets flying in and out of the municipal airport were few and far between these days, but this was a small plane, bumbling along in the unusually clear sky and belching a stream of white from its tail. The plane twisted and banked, rose and fell, the smoke (or whatever chemical it was) forming letters.

"Huh," Gus said, craning. "Skywriting plane. Haven't seen one since I was a kid."

23

CHARLES, the plane wrote. Then KRANTZ. And then—of course—39 GREAT YEARS. The name was already starting to fuzz out as the plane wrote THANKS, CHUCK!

"What the fuck," Gus said.

"My sentiments exactly," Marty said.

He had skipped breakfast, so when he went back inside, Marty microwaved one of his frozen dinners—a Marie Callender's Chicken Pot Pie, quite tasty—and took it into the living room to watch TV. But the only two stations he could pull in were showing the photograph of Charles "Chuck" Krantz sitting at his desk with his pen at the eternal ready. Marty stared at it while he ate his pot pie, then killed the idiot box and went back to bed. It seemed the most sensible thing to do.

He slept for most of the day, and although he didn't dream of her (at least that he could remember), he woke up thinking of Felicia. He wanted to see her, and when he did he would ask if he could sleep over. Maybe even stay. Sixty different varieties of shit, Gus had said, and all at once. If this really was the end, he didn't want to face it alone.

Harvest Acres, the tidy little development where Felicia now lived, was three miles away, and Marty had no intention of risking the drive in his car, so he put on his sweatpants and sneakers. It was a beautiful late afternoon for walking, the sky still an unblemished blue, and plenty of people were out and about. A few looked as if they were enjoying the sunshine, but most just looked down at their feet. There was little talk, even among those who were walking in pairs or trios.

On Park Drive, one of the east side's main thoroughfares, all four lanes were jammed with cars, most of them empty. Marty wove his way between them, and on the other side encountered an elderly man in a tweed suit and matching trilby hat. He was sitting on the curb and knocking his pipe out into the gutter. He saw Marty watching him and smiled.

"Just taking a rest," he said. "I walked downtown to look at the sinkhole and take a few pictures with my phone. Thought one of the local television stations might be interested, but they all seem to be

25

off the air. Except for pictures of that fellow Krantz, that is."

"Yes," Marty said. "It's all Chuck, all the time now. Any idea who—"

"None. I've asked two dozen people, at least. Nobody knows. Our man Krantz appears to be the Oz of the Apocalypse."

Marty laughed. "Where are you heading, sir?"

"Harvest Acres. Nice little enclave. Off the beaten track." He reached into his jacket, produced a pouch of tobacco, and began reloading his pipe.

"I'm going there myself. My ex lives there. Maybe we could walk together."

The elderly gent got up with a wince. "As long as you don't rush along." He lit his pipe, puffing away. "Arthritis. I have pills for it, but the more the arthritis sets in, the less they do."

"Sucks," Marty said. "You set the pace."

The old guy did. It was a slow one. His name was Samuel Yarbrough. He was owner and chief undertaker of the Yarbrough Funeral Home. "But my real interest is meteorology," he said. "Dreamed of being a television weatherman in my salad days, perhaps even on one of

26

the networks, but they all seem to have a pash for young women with . . ." He put his cupped hands in front of his chest. "I keep up, though, read the journals, and I can tell you an amazing thing. If you want to hear."

"Sure."

They came to a bus bench. Stenciled on the back was CHARLES "CHUCK" KRANTZ 39 GREAT YEARS! THANKS, CHUCK! Sam Yarbrough took a seat and patted the space next to him. Marty sat. It was downwind of Yarbrough's pipe, but that was okay. Marty liked the smell.

"Do you know how people say there's twenty-four hours in a day?" Yarbrough asked.

"And seven days in a week. Everybody knows that, even little kids."

"Well, everybody is wrong. There were twenty-three hours and fifty-six minutes in a stellar day. Plus a few odd seconds."

"Were?"

"Correct. Based on my calculations, which I assure you I can back up, there are now twenty-four hours and *two* minutes in a day. Do you know what that means, Mr. Anderson?"

STEPHEN KING

Marty thought it over. "Are you telling me the earth's rotation is slowing down?"

"Exactly." Yarbrough took his pipe out of his mouth and gestured at the people passing them on the sidewalk. Their numbers were thinning now that afternoon had begun to edge into twilight. "I'll bet many of those folks think the multiple disasters we're facing have a single cause rooted in what we have done to the earth's environment. It's not so. I would be the first to admit that we have treated our mother—yes, she's the mother of us all—very badly, certainly molested her if not outright raped her, but we're puny compared to the great clock of the universe. *Puny*. No, whatever is happening is much larger than environmental degradation."

"Maybe it's Chuck Krantz's fault," Marty said.

Yarbrough looked at him in surprise, then laughed. "Back to him, eh? Chuck Krantz is retiring and the entire population of earth, not to mention the earth itself, is retiring with him? Is that your thesis?"

"Got to blame something," Marty said, smiling. "Or someone."

Sam Yarbrough stood up, put a hand to the small of his back, stretched and winced. "With apologies to Mr. Spock, that's illogical. I suppose thirty-nine years is quite a span in terms of human life—almost half—but the last ice age happened quite a bit longer ago. Not to mention the age of the dinosaurs. Shall we mosey?"

They moseyed, their shadows stretching ahead of them. Marty was mentally scolding himself for having slept away the best part of a beautiful day. Yarbrough was moving ever more slowly. When they finally reached the brick arch marking the entrance to Harvest Acres, the old mortician sat down again.

"I think I'll watch the sunset while I wait for the arthritis to settle a bit. Would you care to join me?"

Marty shook his head. "Think I'll go on."

"Check the ex," Yarbrough said. "I understand. It was nice speaking with you, Mr. Anderson."

Marty started beneath the arch, then turned back. "Charles Krantz means *something*," he said. "I'm sure of it."

"You could be right," Sam said, puffing on his pipe, "but the slowing of the earth's rotation . . . nothing's bigger than that, my friend."

29

The central thoroughfare of the Harvest Acres development was a graceful tree-lined parabola from which shorter streets diverged. The streetlights, which looked to Marty like those in illustrated Dickens novels, had come on, casting a moonlight glow. As Marty approached Fern Lane, where Felicia lived, a little girl on roller skates appeared, banking gracefully around the corner. She was wearing baggy red shorts and a sleeveless tee with somebody's face on it, maybe a rock star or a rapper. Marty guessed her age at ten or eleven, and seeing her cheered him enormously. A little girl on roller skates: what could be more normal in this abnormal day? This abnormal *year*?

"Yo," he said.

"Yo," she agreed, but pivoted neatly on her skates, perhaps ready to flee if he turned out to be one of the Chester the Molester types her mother had no doubt warned her about.

"I'm going to see my ex-wife," Marty said, standing where he was. "Felicia Anderson. Or maybe she's back to Gordon now. That was her maiden name. She lives on Fern Lane. Number 19."

The little girl pivoted on her skates, an effortless move that would have left Marty flat on his ass. "Oh yeah, maybe I've seen you before. Blue Prius?"

"That's me."

"If you come to see her, why's she your ex?"

"Still like her."

"You don't fight?"

"We used to. We get along better now that we're exes."

"Miz Gordon gives us gingersnap cookies sometimes. Me and my little brother, Ronnie. I like Oreos better, but . . ."

"But that's the way the cookie crumbles, right?" Marty said.

"Nah, gingersnaps don't crumble. At least not until you crunch em up in your mou—"

At that moment the streetlights went out, turning the main drag into a lagoon of shadows. All the houses went dark at the same time. There had been outages in the city before, some as long as eighteen hours, but the power had always come back. Marty wasn't sure it would this time. Maybe, but he had a feeling that electricity, which he (and everyone else)

31

had taken for granted all his life, might have gone the way of the Internet.

"Booger," said the little girl.

"You better go home," Marty said. "With no streetlights, it's too dark for skating."

"Mister? Is everything going to be all right?"

Although he had no kids of his own, he'd taught them for twenty years and felt that, although you should tell them the truth once they reached the age of sixteen, a kind-hearted lie was often the right way to go when they were as young as this girl. "Sure."

"But look," she said, and pointed.

He followed her trembling finger to the house on the corner of Fern Lane. A face was appearing on the darkened bay window overlooking a small patch of lawn. It appeared in glowing white lines and shadows, like ectoplasm at a séance. Smiling moon face. Black-framed glasses. Pen poised. Over it: CHARLES KRANTZ. Below it: 39 GREAT YEARS! THANKS, CHUCK!

"It's happening to all of them," she whispered.

She was right. Chuck Krantz was rising on the front windows of every house on Fern Lane. Marty turned and saw an arc of Krantz faces stretching out behind him on the main avenue. Dozens of Chucks, maybe hundreds. Thousands, if this phenomenon was happening all over the city.

"Go home," Marty said, not smiling anymore. "Go home to your mom and dad, poppet. Do it right now."

She skated away, her skates rumbling on the sidewalk and her hair flying out behind her. He could see the red shorts, then she was lost in the thickening shadows.

Marty walked quickly in the direction she had gone, observed by the smiling face of Charles "Chuck" Krantz in every window. Chuck in his white shirt and dark tie. It was like being watched by a horde of ghost-clones. Marty was glad there was no moon; what if Chuck's face had appeared there? How would he deal with *that*?

He gave up walking at number 13. He ran the rest of the way to Felicia's little two-room bungalow, pounded up the front walk, and knocked on the door. He waited, suddenly sure she was still at the hospital, maybe working a double, but then he heard her footsteps. The door opened. She was holding a candle. It underlit her frightened face.

33

"Marty, thank God. Do you see them?"

"Yes." The guy was in her front window, too. Chuck. Smiling. Looking like every accountant who ever lived. A man who wouldn't say boo to a goose.

"They just started . . . showing up!"

"I know. I saw."

"Is it just here?"

"I think it's everywhere. I think it's almost—"

Then she was hugging him, pulling him inside, and he was glad she hadn't given him a chance to say the other two words: *the end*.

2

Douglas Beaton, associate professor of philosophy in Ithaca College's Department of Philosophy and Religion, sits in a hospital room, waiting for his brother-in-law to die. The only sounds are the steady *bip . . . bip . . . bip* of the heart monitor and Chuck's slow and increasingly labored breathing. Most of the machinery has been turned off.

"Unc?"

Doug turns to see Brian in the doorway, still wearing his letter jacket and backpack.

"You left school early?" Doug asks.

"With permission. Mom texted me that she was going to let them turn off the machines. Did they?"

"Yes."

"When?"

"An hour ago."

"Where's Mom now?"

"In the chapel on the first floor. She's praying for his soul."

And probably praying that she did the right thing, Doug thinks. Because even when the priest tells you yes, it's fine, let God take care of the rest, it feels wrong somehow.

"I'm supposed to text her if it looks like he's . . ." Brian's uncle shrugs.

Brian approaches the bed and looks down at his father's still white face. With his black-framed glasses put aside, the boy thinks his dad doesn't look old enough to have a son who's a freshman in high school.

35

He looks like a high school kid himself. He picks up his father's hand and plants a brief kiss on the crescent-shaped scar there.

"Guys as young as him aren't supposed to die," Brian says. He speaks softly, as if his father can hear. "Jesus, Uncle Doug, he just turned thirty-nine last winter!"

"Come sit down," Doug says, and pats the empty chair next to him.

"That's Mom's seat."

"When she comes back, you can give it to her."

Brian shucks his backpack and sits down. "How long do you think it will be?"

"The doctors said he could go anytime. Before tomorrow, almost certainly. You know the machines were helping him breathe, right? And there were IVs to feed him. He's not . . . Brian, he's not in any pain. That part is over."

"Glioblastoma," Brian says bitterly. When he turns to his uncle, he's crying. "Why would God take my dad, Uncle Doug? Explain it to me."

"I can't. God's ways are a mystery."

"Well fuck the mystery," the boy says. "Mysteries should stay in storybooks, where they belong."

Uncle Doug nods and puts an arm around Brian's shoulders. "I know it's hard, kiddo, it's hard for me, too, but it's all I got. Life's a mystery. So is death."

They fall silent, listening to the steady *bip . . . bip . . . bip* and the rasp as Charles Krantz—Chuck, to his wife and his wife's brother and his friends—takes one slow breath after another, his body's last interactions with the world, each inhale and exhale managed (like the beat of his heart) by a failing brain where a few operations still continue. The man who spent his working life in the accounting department of the Midwest Trust is now doing his final tallies: small income, large disbursements.

"Banks are supposed to be heartless, but they really loved him there," Brian says. "They sent a ton of flowers. The nurses put them in that solarium thing because he's not supposed to have flowers. What did they think? That it was going to kick off an allergy attack or something?"

"He loved working there," Doug says. "It wasn't a big deal in the grand scheme of things, I suppose—he was never going to win a Nobel Prize or get a Medal of Freedom from the president—but he did love it."

37

"Dancing, too," Brian says. "He loved dancing. He was good. So was Mom—they could really cut a rug, she used to say. But she also said he was better."

Doug laughs. "Used to call himself the poor man's Fred Astaire. And model trains when he was a boy. His zaydee had a set. You know, his granddad?"

"Yeah," Brian says. "I know about his zaydee."

"He had a good life, Bri."

"Not enough of it," Brian says. "He'll never get to take the train across Canada like he wanted to. Or visit Australia—he wanted that, too. He's never going to see me graduate high school. He's never going to have a retirement party where people make funny speeches and give him a gold . . ." He wiped his eyes on the sleeve of his jacket. "A gold watch."

Doug squeezes his nephew's shoulders.

Brian speaks looking down at his clasped hands. "I want to believe in God, Unc, and I sort of do, but I don't understand why it has to be this way. Why God would *let* it be this way. It's a mystery? You're the hot-shot philosophy guy and that's the best you can do?"

Yes, because death brings philosophy to ruin, Doug thinks.

"You know what they say, Brian—death takes the best of us and death takes the rest of us."

Brian tries to smile. "If that's supposed to be comforting, you need to try harder."

Doug seems not to have heard. He's looking at his brother-in-law, who is—in Doug's mind—an actual brother. Who has given his sister a good life. Who helped him get his start in business, and that's really the least of it. They had some fine times together. Not enough, but it looks like they'll have to do.

"The human brain is finite—no more than a sponge of tissue inside a cage of bone—but the mind within the brain is infinite. Its storage capacity is colossal, its imaginative reach beyond our ability to comprehend. I think when a man or woman dies, a whole world falls to ruin—the world that person knew and believed in. Think of that, kiddo—billions of people on earth, and each one of those billions with a world inside. The earth their minds have conceived."

"And now my dad's world is dying."

"But not ours," Doug says, and gives his nephew another squeeze. "Ours will go on a little while longer.

39

And your mother's. We need to be strong for her, Brian. As strong as we can."

They fall silent, looking at the dying man in the hospital bed, listening to the *bip . . . bip . . . bip* of the monitor and the slow breaths Chuck Krantz inhales and exhales. Once it stops. His chest remains flat. Brian tenses. Then it rises again with another of those agonal rasps.

"Text Mom," Brian says. "Right now."

Doug already has his phone out. "Way ahead of you." And types: **Better come, sis. Brian is here. I think Chuck is near the end.**

3

Marty and Felicia went out on the back lawn. They sat in chairs they carried down from the patio. The power was out all over the city now, and the stars were very bright. Brighter than Marty had ever seen them since he was a boy growing up in Nebraska. Back then he'd had a small telescope and conned the universe from his attic window.

"There's Aquila," he said. "The Eagle. There's Cygnus, the Swan. See it?"

"Yes. And there's the North Sta—" She stopped. "Marty? Did you see . . ."

"Yes," he said. "It just went out. And there goes Mars. Goodbye, Red Planet."

"Marty, I'm scared."

Was Gus Wilfong looking up at the sky tonight? Andrea, the woman who'd been on the Neighborhood Watch Committee with Felicia? Samuel Yarbrough, the undertaker? What about the little girl in the red shorts? Star light, star bright, last stars I see tonight.

Marty took her hand. "I am, too."

4

Ginny, Brian, and Doug stand beside Chuck Krantz's bed, their hands joined. They wait as Chuck— husband, father, accountant, dancer, fan of TV crime shows—takes his last two or three breaths.

"Thirty-nine years," Doug says. "Thirty-nine *great* years. Thanks, Chuck."

41

5

Marty and Felicia sat with their faces turned up to the sky, watching the stars go out. First in ones and twos, then by the dozens, then by the hundreds. As the Milky Way rolled away into darkness, Marty turned to his ex-wife.

"I love—"

Black.

ACT II

BUSKERS

With the help of his friend Mac, who has an old van, Jared Franck sets up his drumkit in his favored spot on Boylston Street between Walgreens and the Apple Store. He has a good feeling about today. It's Thursday afternoon, the weather is fucking gorgeous, and the streets are thronged with people looking forward to the weekend, which is always better than the weekend itself. For Thursday afternoon people, that anticipation is pure. Friday afternoon people have to put anticipation aside and get to work having fun.

"All good?" Mac asks him.

"Yes. Thanks."

"My ten per cent is all the thanks I want, bro."

Mac heads out, probably to the comics store, maybe to Barnes & Noble, then to the Common to read whatever he's bought. A big reader is Mac. Jared will call him when it's time to pack up. Mac will bring his van.

45

Jared puts down a battered tophat (scuffed velvet, tattered silk grosgrain band) he bought for seventy-five cents in a secondhand shop in Cambridge, then places the sign in front of it that reads THIS IS A MAGIC HAT! GIVE FREELY AND YOUR CONTRIBUTION WILL DOUBLE! He drops in a couple of dollar bills to give people the right idea. The weather is warm for early October, which allows him to dress as he likes for his Boylston gigs—sleeveless tee with FRANCKLY DRUMS on the front, khaki shorts, ratty Converse hightops without socks—but even on chilly days, he usually shucks his coat if he's wearing one, because when you find the beat, you feel the heat.

Jared unfolds his stool and gives a preparatory paradiddle across the drumheads. A few people glance at him, but most simply sweep on by, lost in their talk of friends, dinner plans, where to get a drink, and the day gone by to the mystery-dump where spent days go.

Meanwhile it's a long time until eight o'clock, which is when a BPD car usually slides over to the curb with a cop leaning out the passenger window to tell him it's time to pack it up. Then he'll call Mac. For now there's money to be made. He sets up his hi-hat and crash cymbal, then adds the cowbell, because it feels like a cowbell kind of day.

Jared and Mac work part-time at Doctor Records on Newbury Street, but on a good day Jared can make almost as much busking. And busk-drumming on sunny Boylston Street is certainly better than the patchouli atmosphere of the Doc's, and long conversations with the record nerds looking for Dave Van Ronk on Folkways or Dead rarities on paisley vinyl. Jared always wants to ask them where they were when Tower Records was going under.

He's a dropout from Juilliard, which he calls—with apologies to Kay Kyser—the Kollege of Musical Knowledge. He lasted three semesters, but in the end it wasn't for him. They wanted you to think about what you were doing, and as far as Jared is concerned, the beat is your friend and thinking is the enemy. He sits in on the occasional gig, but bands don't interest him much. Although he never says it (okay, maybe once or twice, while drunk), he thinks maybe music itself is the enemy. He rarely thinks about these issues

47

once he's in the groove. Once he's in the groove, music is a ghost. Only the drums matter then. The beat.

He starts warming up, going easy at first, slow tempo, no cowbell, no tom and no rimshots, not minding that Magic Hat stays empty except for his two crumpled dollars and a quarter flipped in (contemptuously) by a kid on a skateboard. There is time. There is a way in. Like anticipating the joys of an autumn weekend in Boston, finding the in is half the fun. Maybe even most of it.

Janice Halliday is on her way home from seven hours at Paper and Page, trudging down Boylston with her head lowered and her purse clasped close. She may walk all the way to Fenway before she starts looking for the nearest T station, because right now walking is what she wants. Her boyfriend of sixteen months just broke up with her. Dumped her, not to put too fine a point on it. Kicked her to the curb. He did it the modern way, by text.

We r just not right for each other. ☹
Then: U will always be in my heart! ♥

Then: **Friends 4ever OK?** ☺ ✌️

Not right for each other probably means he met someone and will spend the weekend with her picking apples in New Hampshire and later on fucking in some B&B. He won't see Janice tonight, or ever, in the smart pink blouse and red wrap skirt she's wearing unless she texts him a photo with a message reading **This is what U R missing, you pile of** 💩.

It was totally unexpected, that's what set her back on her heels, like having a door slammed in your face just as you were getting ready to walk through it. The weekend, which seemed full of possibility this morning, now looks to her like the entrance to a hollow, slowly turning barrel into which she must crawl. She's not down to work at P&P on Saturday, but maybe she'll call Maybelline and see if she can pick up Saturday morning, at least. Sunday the store is closed. Sunday best not considered, at least for now.

"Friends forever my ass." She says this to her purse, because she's looking down. She isn't in love with him, never even kidded herself that she was, but it's a dismaying shock, just the same. He was a nice guy (at least she thought so), a pretty good lover, and fun

49

to be with, as they say. Now she's twenty-two and dumped and it sucks. She supposes she'll have some wine when she gets home, and cry. Crying might be good. Therapeutic. Maybe she'll cue up one of her big-band playlists and dance around the room. Dancing with myself, as the Billy Idol song says. She loved to dance in high school, and those Friday night dances were happy times. Maybe she can recapture a little of that happiness.

No, she thinks, those tunes—and those memories— will just make you cry more. High school was a long time ago. This is the real world, where guys break up with you without warning.

Up ahead a couple of blocks, she hears drumming.

Charles Krantz—Chuck, to his friends—makes his way along Boylston Street dressed in the armor of accountancy: gray suit, white shirt, blue tie. His black Samuel Windsor shoes are inexpensive but sturdy. His briefcase swings by his side. He takes no notice of the chattering after-work throngs eddying around him. He's in Boston attending a week-long conference titled Banking in the Twenty-First Century. He has been sent by *his* bank, Midwest Trust, all expenses paid. Very nice, not least because he's never visited Beantown before.

The conference is being held at a hotel that is perfect for accountants, clean and fairly cheap. Chuck has enjoyed the speakers and the panels (he was on one panel and is scheduled to be on another before the conference ends at noon tomorrow), but had no wish to spend his off-duty hours in the company of seventy other accountants. He speaks their language, but likes to think he speaks others, as well. At least he did, although some of the vocabulary is now lost.

Now his sensible Samuel Windsor Oxfords are taking him for an afternoon walk. Not very exciting, but quite pleasant. *Quite pleasant* is enough these days. His life is narrower than the one he once hoped for, but he's made his peace with that. He understands that narrowing is the natural order of things. There comes a time when you realize you're never going to be the President of the United States and settle for being president of the Jaycees instead. And there's a bright side. He has a wife to whom he is scrupulously

51

faithful, and an intelligent, good-humored son in middle school. He also has only nine months to live, although he doesn't know it yet. The seeds of his end—the place where life narrows to a final point— are planted deep, where no surgeon's knife will ever go, and they have lately begun to awaken. Soon they will bear black fruit.

To those passing him—the college girls in their colorful skirts, the college boys with their Red Sox caps turned around, the impeccably dressed Asian Americans from Chinatown, the matrons with their shopping bags, the Vietnam vet holding out a huge ceramic cup with an American flag and the motto THESE COLORS DON'T RUN on its side—Chuck Krantz must surely look like white America personi- fied, buttoned up and tucked in and all about chasing the dollar. He is those things, yes, the industrious ant trundling its preordained path through flocks of pleasure-seeking grasshoppers, but he's other things as well. Or was.

He's thinking about the little sister. Was her name Rachel or Regina? Reba? Renee? He can't remember for sure, only that she was the lead guitarist's little sister.

During his junior year in high school, long before he became an industrious ant working in that hill known as Midwest Trust, Chuck was the lead singer in a band called the Retros. They called themselves that because they played a lot of stuff from the sixties and seventies, heavy on British groups like the Stones and the Searchers and the Clash, because most of those tunes were simple. They steered clear of the Beatles, where the songs were full of weird chords like modified sevenths.

Chuck got to be the lead singer for two reasons: although he couldn't play an instrument he could carry a tune, and his grandpa had an old SUV which he allowed Chuck to drive to gigs, as long as they weren't too far. The Retros were bad to start with, and only mediocre when they broke up at the end of junior year, but they had, as the rhythm guitarist's father once put it, "made that quantum leap to palatability." And really, it was hard to do too much damage when you were playing stuff like "Bits and Pieces" (Dave Clark Five) and "Rockaway Beach" (Ramones).

Chuck's tenor voice was pleasing enough in an unremarkable way, and he wasn't afraid to scream or

53

go falsetto when the occasion called for it, but what he really liked were the instrumental breaks, because then he could dance and strut his way across the stage like Jagger, sometimes wagging the mike stand between his legs in a way he considered suggestive. He could also moonwalk, which always drew applause.

The Retros were a garage band that sometimes practiced in an actual garage and sometimes in the lead guitarist's downstairs rec room. On those latter occasions, the lead's little sister (Ruth? Reagan?) usually came ditty-bopping down the stairs in her Bermuda shorts. She'd station herself between their two Fender amps, waggle her hips and butt in exaggerated fashion, put her fingers in her ears, and stick out her tongue. Once, when they were taking a break, she sidled up to Chuck and whispered, "Just between you and me, you sing like old people fuck."

Charles Krantz, the future accountant, had whispered back, "Like you'd know, monkeybutt."

Little sister ignored this. "I like to watch you dance, though. You do it like a white guy, but still."

Little sister, also white, also liked to dance. Sometimes after practice she would put on one of her homemade cassettes and he'd dance with her while the other guys in the band hooted and made semi-smart remarks, the two of them doing their Michael Jackson moves and laughing like loons.

Chuck's thinking about teaching little sister (Ramona?) how to moonwalk when he first hears the drums. Some guy is banging a basic rock beat that the Retros might have played back in the days of "Hang On Sloopy" and "Brand New Cadillac." At first he thinks it's all in his head, maybe even the start of one of the migraines that have plagued him lately, but then the crowd of pedestrians on the next block clears long enough for him to see a kid in a sleeveless tee, sitting on his little stool and beating out that tasty old-time rhythm.

Chuck thinks, Where's a little sister to dance with when you need one?

Jared has been on the job for ten minutes now and has nothing to show for it but that one sarcastic quarter flipped into Magic Hat by the skateboard kid. It makes no sense to him, on a pleasant Thursday afternoon like this with the weekend just around the bend, he should have at least five dollars in the hat by now. He doesn't need the money to keep from starving, but man doesn't live by food and rent alone. A man has to keep his self-image in order, and drumming here on Boylston is a big part of his. He is onstage. He is performing. Soloing, in fact. What's in the hat is how he judges who is digging the performance and who is not.

He twirls his sticks between his fingertips, sets himself, and plays the intro to "My Sharona," but it's not right. Sounds canned. He sees a Mr. Businessman type coming toward him, briefcase swinging like a short pendulum, and something about him— God knows what—makes Jared want to announce his approach. He slips first into a reggae beat, then something slinkier, like a cross between "I Heard It Through the Grapevine" and "Susie Q."

For the first time since running that quick paradiddle to gauge the sound of his kit, Jared feels a spark and understands why he wanted the cowbell today. He begins to whack it on the offbeat, and what he's drumming morphs into something like that old joint by the Champs, "Tequila." It's pretty cool. The groove has arrived, and the groove is like a road you want to follow. He could speed the beat up, get some tom in there, but he's watching Mr. Businessman, and that seems wrong for this dude. Jared has no idea why Mr. Businessman has become the groove's focal point, and doesn't care. Sometimes it just happens that way. The groove turns into a story. He imagines Mr. Businessman on vacation in one of those places where you get a little pink umbrella in your drink. Maybe he's with his wife, or maybe it's his personal assistant, an ash blond in a turquoise bikini. And this is what they're hearing. This is the drummer warming up for the night's gig, before the tiki torches are lit.

He believes Mr. Businessman will just go past on his way to his Mr. Businessman hotel, the chances that he'll feed Magic Hat hovering somewhere between slim and none. When he's gone, Jared will switch to something else, give the cowbell a rest, but for now this beat is the right one.

But instead of floating on by, Mr. Businessman stops. He's smiling. Jared gives him a grin and nods to the tophat on the pavement, never missing a beat.

Mr. Businessman doesn't seem to notice him, and he doesn't feed the hat. He drops his briefcase between his black Mr. Businessman shoes instead and begins moving his hips side to side with the beat. Just hips: everything else stays still. His face is poker. He seems to be looking at a spot directly over Jared's head.

"Go, man," a young man remarks, and chinks some coins into the hat. For the gently jiving Mr. Businessman, not the beat, but that's okay.

Jared begins working the hi-hat in quick tender strokes, teasing it, almost caressing it. With his other hand he begins knocking the cowbell on the offbeat, using the kick-pedal to add a little bottom. It's nice. The guy in the gray suit looks like a banker, but that hip-sway is something else. He raises a hand and begins ticking his forefinger to the beat. On the back of the hand is a small crescent-shaped scar.

Chuck hears the beat change, becoming a little more exotic, and for a moment he almost comes back to himself and walks away. Then he thinks, Fuck it, no law against dancing a little on the sidewalk. He steps back from his briefcase so he won't trip, then puts his hands on his moving hips and does a jivey clockwise turn like an about-face. It's how he used to do it back in the day, when the band was playing "Satisfaction" or "Walking the Dog." Someone laughs, someone else applauds, and he goes back the other way with the tail of his coat flying. He's thinking about dancing with little sister. Little sister was a booger with a dirty mouth, but she could sure get down on it.

Chuck himself hasn't got down on it—that mystical, satisfying *it*—in years, but every move feels perfect. He lifts one leg and spins on the other heel. Then he clasps his hands behind his back like a schoolboy called on to recite and moonwalks in place on the pavement in front of his briefcase.

The drummer goes "Yow, daddy!" in surprise and delight. He picks up the pace, now going from the cowbell to the floor tom with his left hand, working the kick-pedal, never losing the metallic sighing from the hi-hat. People are gathering. Money is pouring into Magic Hat: paper as well as metal. Something is happening here.

59

Two young men in matching berets and Rainbow Coalition tees are at the front of the little crowd. One of them tosses what looks like a five into the hat and yells "Go, man, go!"

Chuck doesn't need the encouragement. He's into it now. Banking in the twenty-first century has slipped his mind. He frees the button on his suit coat, brushes the coat behind him with the backs of his hands, hooks his thumbs into his belt like a gunslinger, and does a modified split, out and back. He follows with a quick-step and turn. The drummer is laughing and nodding. "You the cheese," he says. "You the cheese, daddy!"

The crowd is growing, the hat is filling, Chuck's heart isn't just beating in his chest but thrumming. Good way to have a heart attack, but he doesn't care. If his wife saw him doing this she'd shit a brick, and he doesn't care. His son would be embarrassed, but his son isn't here. He puts his right shoe on his left calf, spins again, and when he comes back front and center, he sees a pretty young woman standing next to the beret guys. She's wearing a filmy pink blouse and a red wrap skirt. She's staring at him with wide, fascinated eyes.

Chuck holds his hands out to her, smiling, snapping his fingers. "Come on," he says. "Come on, little sister, dance."

Jared doesn't think she will—she looks like the shy type—but she walks slowly toward the man in the gray suit. Maybe Magic Hat really is magic.

"Dance!" one of the beret guys says, and others pick it up, clapping along with the beat Jared is laying down: "Dance, dance, dance!"

Janice breaks into a what-the-hell smile, tosses her purse down beside Chuck's briefcase, and takes his hands. Jared drops what he's been doing and turns into Charlie Watts, hammering like a soldier. Mr. Businessman twirls the girl, puts a hand on her trim waist, draws her to him, and quick-steps her past the drumkit, almost to the corner of the Walgreens building. Janice pulls away, waving her finger in a "naughty-naughty" gesture, then comes back and grasps both of Chuck's hands. As if they had practiced this a hundred times, he does another modified split and she shoots between his legs, a daring move that

61

opens the wrap skirt to the top of one pretty thigh. There are a few gasps as she props herself on one tented hand and then springs back up. She's laughing.

"No more," Chuck says, patting his chest. "I can't—"

She springs to him and puts her hands on his shoulders and he can after all. He catches her by the waist, turning her on his hip and then setting her neatly on the pavement. He lifts her left hand and she spins beneath it like a hopped-up ballerina. There must be over a hundred people watching now, they crowd the sidewalk and spill into the street. They burst into fresh applause.

Jared runs the drums one time, hits the cymbals, then holds up his sticks triumphantly. There's another round of applause. Chuck and Janice are looking at each other, both out of breath. Chuck's hair, just starting to gray, is stuck to his sweaty forehead.

"What are we doing?" Janice asks. Now that the drums have stopped, she looks dazed.

"I don't know," Chuck says, "but that's the best thing that's happened to me in I don't know how long."

Magic Hat is full to overflowing.

"More!" someone shouts, and the crowd picks it up. There are many phones being held up, ready to catch the next dance, and the girl looks like she would, but she's young. Chuck is danced out. He looks at the drummer and shakes his head. The drummer gives him a nod to show he understands. Chuck is wondering how many people were quick enough to video that first dance, and what his wife will think if she sees it. Or his son. And suppose it goes viral? Unlikely, but if it does, if it gets back to the bank, what will they think when they see the man they sent to a conference in Boston shaking his booty on Boylston Street with a woman young enough to be his daughter? Or somebody's little sister. Just what did he think he was doing?

"No more, folks," the drummer calls. "We gotta quit while we're ahead."

"And I need to get home," the girl says.

"Not yet," says the drummer. "Please."

Twenty minutes later they're sitting on a bench facing the duck pond in Boston Common. Jared called Mac.

63

Chuck and Janice helped Jared pack up his kit and load it in the back of the van. A few people hung out, congratulating them, offering high fives, adding a few more bucks to the overflowing hat. When they're rolling—Chuck and Janice sitting side by side in the back seat, their feet planted among stacks of comic books—Mac says they'll never find parking next to the Common.

"We will today," Jared says. "Today is magic." And they do, right across from the Four Seasons.

Jared counts out the cash. Somebody has actually tossed in a fifty, maybe the beret guy mistaking it for a five. There's over four hundred dollars in all. Jared has never had such a day. Never expected to. He sets aside Mac's ten per cent (Mac is currently standing at the edge of the pond, feeding the ducks from a package of peanut butter crackers he happened to have in his pocket), then begins to divvy up the rest.

"Oh, no," Janice says when she understands what he's doing. "That's yours."

Jared shakes his head. "Nope, we split even. By myself I wouldn't have made half this much even if I drummed until midnight." Not that the cops would ever allow such a thing. "Sometimes I clear thirty bucks, and that's on a good day."

Chuck has the beginnings of one of his headaches and knows it's apt to be bad by nine o'clock, but the young man's earnestness makes him laugh just the same. "All right. I don't need it, but I guess I earned it." He reaches out and pats Janice's cheek, just as he sometimes used to pat the cheek of the lead singer's potty-mouthed little sister. "So did you, young lady."

"Where did you learn to dance like that?" Jared asks Chuck.

"Well, there was an extracurricular called Twirlers and Spinners back in middle school, but it was my grandma who showed me the best moves."

"You?" he asks Janice.

"Pretty much the same," she says, and blushes. "High school dances. Where did you learn to drum?"

"Self-taught. Like you," he says to Chuck. "You were great by yourself, man, but the chick added a whole extra dimension. We could do this for a living, you know it? I really think we could busk our way to fame and fortune."

For a mad moment Chuck actually considers it, and sees the girl is, too. Not in a serious way, but in the way you daydream of an alternate life. One where you play pro baseball or climb Mount Everest or duet with Bruce Springsteen at a stadium concert. Then Chuck laughs some more and shakes his head. As the girl tucks her third of the take into her purse, she is also laughing.

"It was really all you," Jared says to Chuck. "What made you stop in front of me? And what made you start moving?"

Chuck thinks that over, then shrugs. He could say it was because he was thinking about that old half-assed band, the Retros, and how he liked to dance across the stage during the instrumental breaks, showing off, swinging that mike stand between his legs, but that's not it. And really, had he ever danced with such elan and freedom even back then, when he had been a teenager, young and limber, with no headaches and nothing to lose?

"It was magic," Janice says. She giggles. She didn't expect to hear that sound coming from her today. Crying, yes. Giggling, no. "Like your hat."

Mac comes back. "Jere, we gotta roll or you're gonna end up spending your take paying for my parking ticket."

Jared stands up. "Sure you don't want to change career streams, you two? We could busk this town from Beacon Hill to Roxbury. Make a name for ourselves."

"I've got a conference to attend tomorrow," Chuck says. "On Saturday I'm flying home. I've got a wife and son waiting for me."

"And I can't do it by myself," Janice says, smiling. "It would be like Ginger without Fred."

"I hear that," Jared says, and holds out his arms. "But you have to get in here before you go. Group hug."

They join him. Chuck knows they can smell his sweat—this suit will have to be dry-cleaned before he wears it again, and strenuously—and he can smell theirs. It's all right. He thinks the girl nailed it when she used the word magic. Sometimes there is such a thing. Not much, but a little. Like finding a forgotten twenty in the pocket of an old coat.

"Buskers forever," Jared says.

Chuck Krantz and Janice Halliday repeat it.

"Buskers forever," Mac says, "great. Now let's get out of here before a meter maid shows up, Jere."

Chuck tells Janice he's headed to the Boston Hotel, past the Prudential Center, if she's going that way. Janice was, the plan had been to walk all the way to Fenway, brooding about her ex-boyfriend and muttering doleful shit to her purse, but she's changed her mind. She says she'll take the T from Arlington Street.

He walks her there, the two of them cutting across the park. At the head of the stairs, she turns to him and says, "Thank you for the dance."

He gives her a bow. "It was my pleasure."

He watches her until she's out of sight, then heads back down Boylston. He walks slowly because his back hurts, his legs hurt, and his head is throbbing. He can't remember having bad headaches like this in his whole life. Not until a couple of months ago, that is. He supposes if they keep up, he'll have to see a doctor. He supposes he knows what this might be.

All that's for later, though. If at all. Tonight he thinks he'll treat himself to a good dinner—why not, he's earned it—and a glass of wine. On second thought, make it Evian. Wine might intensify his headache. When he's finished his meal—dessert definitely included—he'll call Ginny and tell her that her husband might be the next one-day Internet sensation. That probably won't happen, somewhere right now someone is undoubtedly filming a dog juggling empty soda bottles and someone else is memorializing a goat smoking a cigar, but it's better to get out front with it, just in case.

As he passes the place where Jared set up his drums, those two questions recur: Why did you stop to listen, and why did you start to dance? He doesn't know, and would answers make a good thing better?

Later he will lose the ability to walk, never mind dancing with little sister on Boylston Street. Later he will lose the ability to chew food, and his meals will come from a blender. Later he will lose his grip on the difference between waking and sleeping and enter a land of pain so great that he will wonder why God made the world. Later he will forget his wife's name. What he will remember—occasionally—is how he stopped, and dropped his briefcase, and began to move his hips to the beat of the drums, and he will think that is why God made the world. Just that.

ACT I

I CONTAIN MULTITUDES

1

Chuck was looking forward to having a baby sister. His mother promised he could hold her if he was very careful. Of course he was also looking forward to having parents, but none of that worked out thanks to an icy patch on an I-95 overpass. Much later, in college, he would tell a girlfriend that there were all sorts of novels, movies, and TV shows where a main character's parents died in a car crash, but he was the only person he knew who'd had that happen in real life.

The girlfriend thought this over, then rendered her verdict. "I'm sure it happens all the time, although parents can also be taken in housefires, tornadoes, hurricanes, earthquakes, and avalanches while on ski vacations. To name only a few of the possibilities. And what makes you think you're a main character in anything but your own mind?"

She was a poet and sort of a nihilist. The relationship only lasted a semester.

Chuck wasn't in the car when it went flying upside-down from the turnpike overpass because his parents were having a dinner date and he was being babysat by his grandparents, who at that time he was still calling Zaydee and Bubbie (this mostly ended in the third grade, when kids made fun of him and he reverted to the more all-American Grandma and Grandpa). Albie and Sarah Krantz lived just a mile down the road, and it was natural enough for them to raise him after the accident when he became what he first believed to be an orphant. He was seven.

For a year—maybe a year and a half—that was a house of unadulterated sadness. The Krantzes had not only lost their son and daughter-in-law, they had lost the granddaughter who would have been born just three months later. The name had already been picked out: Alyssa. When Chuck said that sounded to him like rain, his mother had laughed and cried at the same time.

He never forgot that.

He knew his other grandparents of course, there were visits every summer, but they were basically strangers to him. They called a lot after he became an orphant, your basic how-are-you-doing-how's-school calls, and the summer visits continued; Sarah (aka Bubbie, aka Grandma) took him on the plane. But his mother's parents remained strangers, living in the foreign land of Omaha. They sent him presents on his birthday and at Christmas—the latter especially nice since Grandma and Grandpa didn't "do" Christmas—but otherwise he continued to think of them as outliers, like the teachers who were left behind as he moved up through the grades.

Chuck began to slip his metaphorical mourning garments first, necessarily pulling his grandparents (old, yeah, but not *ancient*) out of their own grief. There came a time, when Chuck was ten, that they took the boy to Disney World. They had adjoining rooms at the Swan Resort, the door between the rooms kept open at night, and Chuck only heard his grandma crying once. Mostly, they had fun.

75

Some of that good feeling came back home with them. Chuck sometimes heard Grandma humming in the kitchen, or singing along with the radio. There had been lots of take-out meals after the accident (and whole recyclable bins full of Grandpa's Budweiser bottles), but in the year after Disney World, Grandma began cooking again. Good meals that put weight on a formerly skinny boy.

She liked rock and roll while she was cooking, music Chuck would have thought much too young for her, but which she clearly enjoyed. If Chuck wandered into the kitchen looking for a cookie or maybe hoping to make a brown-sugar roll-up with a slice of Wonder Bread, Grandma was apt to hold out her hands to him and start snapping her fingers. "Dance with me, Henry," she'd say.

His name was Chuck, not Henry, but he usually took her up on it. She taught him jitterbug steps and a couple of crossover moves. She told him there were more, but her back was too creaky to attempt them. "I can show you, though," she said, and one Saturday brought back a stack of videotapes from the Blockbuster store. There was *Swing Time*, with

76

Fred Astaire and Ginger Rogers, *West Side Story*, and Chuck's favorite, *Singin' in the Rain*, where Gene Kelly danced with a lamppost.

"You could learn those moves," she said. "You're a natural, kiddo."

He asked her once, when they were drinking iced tea after an especially strenuous go to Jackie Wilson's "Higher and Higher," what she had been like in high school.

"I was a *kusit*," she said. "But don't tell your zaydee I said that. He's old-school, that one."

Chuck never told.

And he never went in the cupola.

Not then.

He asked about it, of course, and more than once. What was up there, what you could see from the high window, why the room was locked. Grandma said it was because the floor wasn't safe and he might go right through it. Grandpa said the same thing, that there was nothing up there because of the rotten floor, and the only thing you could see from those windows was a shopping center, big deal. He said that until one night, just before Chuck's

77

eleventh birthday, when he told at least part of the truth.

2

Drinking is not good for secrets, everybody knows that, and after the death of his son, daughter-in-law, and granddaughter-to-be (Alyssa, sounds like rain), Albie Krantz drank a great deal. He should have bought stock in Anheuser-Busch, that was how much he drank. He could do it because he was retired, and comfortably off, and very depressed.

After the trip to Disney World the drinking tapered off to a glass of wine with dinner or a beer in front of a baseball game. Mostly. Once in awhile—every month at first, every couple of months later on—Chuck's grandpa tied one on. Always at home, and never making any fuss about it. The next day he would move slowly and eat little until afternoon, then he was back to normal.

One night while watching the Red Sox get thumped by the Yankees, when Albie was well into his second sixpack of Bud, Chuck once more raised the subject of the cupola. Mostly just to have something to talk about. With the Sox down by nine, the game wasn't exactly holding his attention.

"I bet you can see way past the Westford Mall," Chuck said.

Grandpa considered this, then pushed the mute button on the TV controller, silencing an ad for Ford Truck Month. (Grandpa said Ford stood for Fix Or Repair Daily.) "If you went up there you might see a lot more than you wanted," he said. "That's why it's locked, boychick."

Chuck felt a small and not entirely unpleasurable chill go through him, and his mind immediately flashed to Scooby-Doo and his friends, chasing down spooks in the Mystery Machine. He wanted to ask what Grandpa meant, but the adult part of him—not there in person, no, not at ten, but something that had begun to speak on rare occasions—told him to be quiet. Be quiet and wait.

"Do you know what style this house is, Chucky?"

"Victorian," Chuck said.

"That's right, and not pretend Victorian, either.

It was built in 1885, been remodeled half a dozen times since, but the cupola was there from the start. Your bubbie and I bought it when the shoe business really took off, and we got it for a song. Been here since 1971, and in all those years I haven't been up to that damn cupola half a dozen times."

"Because the floor's rotted?" Chuck asked, with what he hoped was appealing innocence.

"Because it's full of ghosts," Grandpa said, and Chuck felt that chill again. Not so pleasurable this time. Although Grandpa might be joking. He *did* joke from time to time these days. Jokes were to Grandpa what dancing was to Grandma. He tipped his beer. Belched. His eyes were red. "Christmas Yet to Come. Do you remember that one, Chucky?"

Chuck did, they watched *A Christmas Carol* every year on Christmas Eve even though they didn't "do" Christmas otherwise, but that didn't mean he knew what his grandpa was talking about.

"The Jefferies boy was only a short time later," Grandpa said. He was looking at the TV, but Chuck didn't think he was actually seeing it. "What happened to Henry Peterson . . . that took longer. It was four, maybe five years on. By then I'd almost forgotten what I saw up there." He jerked a thumb at the ceiling. "I said I'd never go up there again after that, and I wish I hadn't. Because of Sarah—your bubbie—and the bread. It's the waiting, Chucky, that's the hard part. You'll find that out when you're—"

The kitchen door opened. It was Grandma, back from Mrs. Stanley's across the street. Grandma had taken her chicken soup because Mrs. Stanley was feeling poorly. So Grandma said anyway, but even at not quite eleven, Chuck had a good idea there was another reason. Mrs. Stanley knew all the neighborhood gossip ("She's a *yente*, that one," Grandpa said), and was always willing to share. Grandma poured all the news out to Grandpa, usually after inviting Chuck out of the room. But out of the room didn't mean out of earshot.

"Who was Henry Peterson, Grandpa?" Chuck asked.

But Grandpa had heard his wife come in. He straightened up in his chair and put his can of Bud aside. "Look at that!" he cried in a passable imitation of sobriety (not that Grandma would be fooled). "The Sox have got the bases loaded!"

81

3

In the top of the eighth, Grandma sent Grandpa down to the Zoney's Go-Mart at the bottom of the block to get milk for Chuck's Apple Jacks in the morning. "And don't even think of driving. The walk will sober you up."

Grandpa didn't argue. With Grandma he rarely did, and when he gave it a try, the results weren't good. When he was gone, Grandma—Bubbie—sat down next to Chuck on the couch and put an arm around him. Chuck put his head on her comfortably padded shoulder. "Was he blabbing to you about his ghosts? The ones that live in the cupola?"

"Um, yeah." There was no point in telling a lie; Grandma saw right through those. "Are there? Have you seen them?"

Grandma snorted. "What do you think, *hantel*?" Later it would occur to Chuck that this wasn't an answer. "I wouldn't pay too much attention to Zaydee. He's a good man, but sometimes he drinks a little too much. Then he rides his hobby horses. I'm sure you know what I'm talking about."

Chuck did. Nixon should have gone to jail; the *faygelehs* were taking over American culture and turning it pink; the Miss America pageant (which Grandma loved) was your basic meat-show. But he had never said anything about ghosts in the cupola before that night. At least to Chuck.

"Bubbie, who was the Jefferies boy?"

She sighed. "That was a very sad thing, boy-chuck." (This was her little joke.) "He lived on the next block over and got hit by a drunk driver when he chased a ball into the street. It happened a long time ago. If your grandpa told you he saw it before it happened, he was mistaken. Or making it up for one of his jokes."

Grandma knew when Chuck was lying; on that night Chuck discovered that was a talent that could go both ways. It was all in the way she stopped looking at him and shifted her eyes to the television, as if what was going on there was interesting, when Chuck knew Grandma didn't give a hang for baseball, not even the World Series.

"He just drinks too much," Grandma said, and that was the end of it.

83

Maybe true. *Probably* true. But after that, Chuck was frightened of the cupola, with its locked door at the top of a short (six steps) flight of narrow stairs lit by a single bare bulb hanging on a black cord. But fascination is fear's twin brother, and sometimes after that night, if both of his grandparents were out, he dared himself to climb them. He would touch the Yale padlock, wincing if it rattled (a sound that might disturb the ghosts pent up inside), then hurry back down the stairs, looking over his shoulder as he went. It was easy to imagine the lock popping open and dropping to the floor. The door creaking open on its unused hinges. If that happened, he guessed he might die of fright.

4

The cellar, on the other hand, wasn't a bit scary. It was brightly lighted by fluorescents. After selling his shoe stores and retiring, Grandpa spent a lot of time down there doing woodwork. It always smelled sweetly of sawdust. In one corner, far from the planers and sanders and the bandsaw he was forbidden to touch, Chuck found a box of Grandpa's Hardy Boys books. They were old-timey but pretty good. He was reading *The Sinister Signpost* one day in the kitchen, waiting for Grandma to remove a batch of cookies from the oven, when she grabbed the book out of his hands.

"You can do better than that," she said. "Time to step up your game, boychuck. Wait right there."

"I was just getting to the good part," Chuck said.

She snorted, a sound to which only Jewish bubbies do true justice. "There are no good parts in these," she said, and took the book away.

What she came back with was *The Murder of Roger Ackroyd*. "Now *this* is a good mystery story," she said. "No dummocks teenagers running around in jalopies. Consider this your introduction to actual writing." She considered. "Okay, so not Saul Bellow, but not bad."

Chuck started the book just to please Grandma, and was soon lost. In his eleventh year he read almost two dozen Agatha Christies. He tried a couple about Miss Marple, but he was much fonder of Hercule

85

Poirot with his fussy mustache and little gray cells. Poirot was one thinking cat. One day, during his summer vacation, Chuck was reading *Murder on the Orient Express* in the backyard hammock and happened to glance up at the window of the cupola far above. He wondered how Monsieur Poirot would go about investigating it.

Aha, he thought. And then *Voilà*, which was better.

The next time Grandma made blueberry muffins, Chuck asked if he could take some to Mrs. Stanley.

"That's very thoughtful of you," Grandma said. "Why don't you do that? Just remember to look both ways when you cross the street." She always told him that when he was going somewhere. Now, with his little gray cells engaged, he wondered if she was thinking of the Jefferies boy.

Grandma was plump (and getting plumper), but Mrs. Stanley was twice her size, a widow who wheezed like a leaky tire when she walked and always seemed to be dressed in the same pink silk wrapper. Chuck felt vaguely guilty about bringing her treats that would add to her girth, but he needed information.

She thanked him for the muffins and asked—as he'd been pretty sure she would—if he would like to have one with her in the kitchen. "I could make tea!"

"Thank you," Chuck said. "I don't drink tea, but I wouldn't mind a glass of milk."

When they were seated at the little kitchen table in a flood of June sunshine, Mrs. Stanley asked how things were going with Albie and Sarah. Chuck, mindful that anything he said in this kitchen would be on the street before the day was out, said they were doing fine. But because Poirot said you had to give a little if you wanted to get a little, he added that Grandma was collecting clothes for the Lutheran homeless shelter.

"Your gramma's a saint," Mrs. Stanley said, obviously disappointed there wasn't more. "What about your granddad? Did he get that thing on his back looked at?"

"Yeah," Chuck said. He took a sip of milk. "The doctor took it off and had it tested. It wasn't one of the bad ones."

"Thank God for that!"

"Yes," Chuck agreed. Having given, he now felt

entitled to get. "He was talking with Grandma about someone named Henry Peterson. I guess he's dead."

He was prepared for disappointment; she might have never heard of Henry Peterson. But Mrs. Stanley widened her eyes until Chuck was actually afraid they might fall out, and grasped her neck like she had a piece of blueberry muffin stuck in there. "Oh, that was so sad! So *awful*! He was the bookkeeper who did your father's accounts, you know. Other companies, too." She leaned forward, her wrapper giving Chuck a view of a bosom so large it seemed hallucinatory. She was still clutching her neck. "*He killed himself,*" she whispered. "*Hung* himself!"

"Was he embezzling?" Chuck asked. There was a lot of embezzling in Agatha Christie books. Also blackmail.

"What? God, no!" She pressed her lips together, as if to keep in something not fit for the ears of such a beardless youth as the one sitting across from her. If that was the case, her natural proclivity to tell everything (and to anyone) prevailed. "His wife ran away with a younger man! Hardly old enough to vote, *and she was in her forties*! What do you think of that?"

The only reply Chuck could think of right off the bat was "Wow!" and that seemed to suffice.

Back at home he pulled his notebook off the shelf and jotted, *G. saw ghost of Jefferies boy <u>not long before he died</u>. Saw ghost of H. Peterson <u>4 or 5 YEARS before he died</u>.* Chuck stopped, chewing the end of his Bic, troubled. He didn't want to write what was in his mind, but felt that as a good detective he had to.

Sarah and the bread. <u>DID HE SEE GRANDMA'S GHOST IN THE CUPOLA???</u>

The answer seemed obvious to him. Why else would Grandpa have talked about how hard the waiting was?

Now I'm waiting, too, Chuck thought. And hoping that it's all just a bunch of bullshit.

5

On the last day of sixth grade, Miss Richards—a sweet, hippy-dippyish young woman who had no command of discipline and would probably not last long in the public education system—tried to read Chuck's class

89

some verses of Walt Whitman's "Song of Myself." It didn't go well. The kids were rowdy and didn't want poetry, only to escape into the months of summer stretching ahead. Chuck was the same, happy to throw spitballs or give Mike Enderby the finger when Miss Richards was looking down at her book, but one line clanged in his head and made him sit up straight.

When the class was finally over and the kids set free, he lingered. Miss Richards sat at her desk and blew a strand of hair back from her forehead. When she saw Chuck still standing there, she gave him a weary smile. "*That* went well, don't you think?"

Chuck knew sarcasm when he heard it, even when the sarcasm was gentle and self-directed. He was Jewish, after all. Well, half.

"What does that mean when he says 'I am large, I contain multitudes'?"

That made her smile perk up. She propped one small fist on her chin and looked at him with her pretty gray eyes. "What do you think it means?"

"All the people he knows?" Chuck ventured.

"Yes," she agreed, "but maybe he means even more. Lean forward."

He leaned over her desk, where *American Verse* lay on top of her grade book. Very gently, she put her palms to his temples. They were cool. They felt so wonderful he had to suppress a shiver. "What's in there between my hands? Just the people you know?"

"More," Chuck said. He was thinking of his mother and father and the baby he never got a chance to hold. Alyssa, sounds like rain. "Memories."

"Yes," she said. "Everything you see. Everything you know. The *world*, Chucky. Planes in the sky, manhole covers in the street. Every year you live, that world inside your head will get bigger and brighter, more detailed and complex. Do you understand?"

"I think so," Chuck said. He was overwhelmed with the thought of a whole world inside the fragile bowl of his skull. He thought of the Jefferies boy, hit in the street. He thought of Henry Peterson, his father's bookkeeper, dead at the end of a rope (he'd had nightmares about that). Their worlds going dark. Like a room when you turned out the light.

Miss Richards took her hands away. She looked concerned. "Are you all right, Chucky?"

"Yes," he said.

91

"Then go on. You're a good boy. I've enjoyed having you in class."

He went to the door, then turned back. "Miss Richards, do you believe in ghosts?"

She considered this. "I believe memories *are* ghosts. But spooks flapping along the halls of musty castles? I think those only exist in books and movies."

And maybe in the cupola of Grandpa's house, Chuck thought.

"Enjoy your summer, Chucky."

6

Chuck did enjoy his summer until August, when Grandma died. It happened down the street, in public, which was a little undignified, but at least it was the kind of death where people can safely say "Thank God she didn't suffer" at the funeral. That other standby, "She had a long, full life" was in more of a gray area; Sarah Krantz had yet to reach her mid-sixties, although she was getting close.

Once more the house on Pilchard Street was one

of unadulterated sadness, only this time there was no trip to Disney World to mark the beginning of recovery. Chuck reverted to calling Grandma his bubbie, at least in his own head, and cried himself to sleep on many nights. He did it with his face in his pillow so he wouldn't make Grandpa feel even worse. Sometimes he whispered, "Bubbie I miss you, Bubbie I love you," until sleep finally took him.

Grandpa wore his mourning band, and lost weight, and stopped telling his jokes, and began to look older than his seventy years, but Chuck also sensed (or thought he did) some relief in his grandpa. If so, Chuck could understand. When you lived with dread day in and day out, there had to be relief when the dreaded thing finally happened and was over. Didn't there?

He didn't go up the steps to the cupola after she died, daring himself to touch the padlock, but he did go down to Zoney's one day just before starting seventh grade at Acker Park Middle School. He bought a soda and a Kit Kat bar, then asked the clerk where the woman was when she had her stroke and died. The clerk, an over-tatted twentysomething with a lot of greased-back blond hair, gave an unpleasant laugh. "Kid, that's a little creepy. Are you, I don't know, brushing up on your serial-killer skills early?"

"She was my grandma," Chuck said. "My bubbie. I was at the community pool when it happened. I came back in the house calling for her and Grandpa told me she was dead."

That wiped the smile off the clerk's face. "Oh, man. I'm sorry. It was over there. Third aisle."

Chuck went to the third aisle and looked, already knowing what he would see.

"She was getting a loaf of bread," the clerk said. "Pulled down almost everything on the shelf when she collapsed. Sorry if that's too much information."

"No," Chuck said, and thought, That's information I already knew.

7

On his second day at Acker Park Middle, Chuck walked past the bulletin board by the main office, then doubled back. Among the posters for Pep Club,

Band, and tryouts for the fall sports teams, there was one showing a boy and girl caught in mid-dance step, he holding his hand up so she could spin beneath. LEARN TO DANCE! it said above the smiling children, in rainbow letters. Below it: JOIN TWIRLERS AND SPINNERS! FALL FLING IS COMING! GET OUT ON THE FLOOR!

An image of painful clarity came to Chuck as he looked at this: Grandma in the kitchen, holding her hands out. Snapping her fingers and saying, "Dance with me, Henry."

That afternoon he went down to the gymnasium, where he and nine hesitant others were greeted enthusiastically by Miss Rohrbacher, the girls' phys ed teacher. Chuck was one of three boys. There were seven girls. All the girls were taller.

One of the boys, Paul Mulford, tried to creep out as soon as he realized he was the smallest kid there, coming in at five-feet-nothing. Miss Rohrbacher chased him down and hauled him back, laughing cheerfully. "No-no-no," said she, "you're *mine* now."

So he was. So they all were. Miss Rohrbacher was the dance-monster, and none could stand in her

95

way. She fired up her boombox and showed them the waltz (Chuck knew it), the cha-cha (Chuck knew it), the ball change (Chuck knew it), then the samba. Chuck didn't know that one, but when Miss Rohrbacher put on "Tequila," by the Champs, and showed them the basic moves, he got it at once and fell in love with it.

He was by far the best dancer in the little club, so Miss Rohrbacher mostly put him with the girls who were clumsy. He understood she did it to make them better, and he was a good sport about it, but it was sort of boring.

Near the end of their forty-five minutes, however, the dance-monster would show mercy and pair him with Cat McCoy, who was an eighth-grader and the best dancer of the girls. Chuck didn't expect romance—Cat was not only gorgeous, she was four inches taller than he was—but he loved to dance with her, and the feeling was mutual. When they got together, they caught the rhythm and let it fill them. They looked into each other's eyes (she had to look down, which was a bummer, but hey—it was what it was) and laughed for the joy of it.

Before letting the kids go, Miss Rohrbacher paired them up (four of the girls had to dance with each other) and told them to freestyle. As they lost their inhibitions and awkwardness, they all got pretty good at it, although most of them were never going to dance at the Copacabana.

One day—this was in October, only a week or so before the Fall Fling—Miss Rohrbacher put on "Billie Jean."

"Watch this," Chuck said, and did a very passable moonwalk. The kids oohed. Miss Rohrbacher's mouth dropped open.

"Oh my God," Cat said. "Show me how you did that!"

He did it again. Cat tried, but the illusion of walking backward just wasn't there.

"Kick off your shoes," Chuck said. "Do it in your socks. Slide into it."

Cat did. It was much better, and they all applauded. Miss Rohrbacher had a go, then all of the others were moonwalking like crazy. Even Dylan Masterson, the clumsiest of them, got into it. Twirlers and Spinners let out half an hour later than usual that day.

97

Chuck and Cat walked out together. "We should do it at the Fling," she said.

Chuck, who hadn't been planning on going, stopped and looked at her with his eyebrows raised.

"Not as a date or anything," Cat hastened on, "I'm going out with Dougie Wentworth—" This Chuck knew. "—but that doesn't mean we couldn't show them some cool moves. I want to, don't you?"

"I don't know," Chuck said. "I'm a lot shorter. I think people would laugh."

"Got you covered," Cat said. "My brother's got a pair of Cuban heels, and I think they'd fit you. You've got big feet for a little kid."

"Thanks a bunch," Chuck said.

She laughed and gave him a sisterly hug.

At the next meeting of Twirlers and Spinners, Cat McCoy brought her brother's Cubans. Chuck, who had already endured slights to his manhood for being in the dance club, was prepared to hate them, but it was love at first sight. The heels were high, the toes were pointed, and they were as black as midnight in Moscow. They looked a lot like the ones Bo Diddley wore back in the day. So okay, they *were* a little big, but toilet paper stuffed into those pointy toes took care of that. Best of all . . . man, they were *slick*. During freestyle, when Miss Rohrbacher put on "Caribbean Queen," the gym floor felt like ice.

"You put scratches on that floor, the janitors will beat your butt," Tammy Underwood said. She was probably right, but there were no scratches. He was too light on his feet to leave any.

8

Chuck went stag to the Fall Fling, which turned out just fine, because all the girls from Twirlers and Spinners wanted to dance with him. Especially Cat, because her boyfriend, Dougie Wentworth, had two left feet and spent most of the evening slouched against the wall with his buddies, all of them sucking up punch and watching the dancers with lordly sneers.

Cat kept asking him when they were going to do their stuff, and Chuck kept putting her off. He said

99

he'd know the right tune when he heard it. It was his bubbie he was thinking of.

Around nine o'clock, half an hour or so before the dance was scheduled to end, the right tune came up. It was Jackie Wilson, singing "Higher and Higher." Chuck strutted to Cat with his hands out. She kicked off her shoes, and with Chuck in her brother's Cubans, they were at least close to the same height. They went out on the floor, and when they did a double moonwalk, they cleared it. The kids made a circle around them and began clapping. Miss Rohrbacher, one of the chaperones, was among them, clapping along with the rest and shouting "Go, go, go!"

They did. As Jackie Wilson shouted that happy, gospel-tinged tune, they danced like Fred Astaire, Ginger Rogers, Gene Kelly, and Jennifer Beals all rolled up into one. They finished with Cat spinning first one way, then the other, then collapsing backward into Chuck's arms with her own held out in a dying swan. He went down in a split that miraculously didn't rip the crotch out of his pants. Two hundred kids cheered when Cat turned her head and put a kiss on the corner of Chuck's mouth.

"One more time!" some kid shouted, but Chuck and Cat shook their heads. They were young, but smart enough to know when to quit. The best cannot be topped.

9

Six months before he died of a brain tumor (at the unfair age of thirty-nine), and while his mind was still working (mostly), Chuck told his wife the truth about the scar on the back of his hand. It wasn't a big deal and hadn't been a big lie, but he'd reached a time in his rapidly diminishing life when it seemed important to clear the books. The only time she'd asked about it (it really was a very small scar), he told her that he had gotten it from a boy named Doug Wentworth, who was pissed about him cavorting with his girl-friend at a middle school dance and pushed him into a chainlink fence outside the gymnasium.

"What actually happened?" Ginny asked, not because it was important to her but because it seemed to be important to him. She didn't care much about

101

whatever had happened to him in middle school. The doctors said he would probably be dead before Christmas. That was what mattered to her.

When their fabulous dance was over and the DJ put on another, more recent tune, Cat McCoy had run to her girlfriends, who giggled and shrieked and hugged her with a fervency of which only thirteen-year-old girls may be capable. Chuck was sweaty and so hot his cheeks felt on the verge of catching fire. He was also euphoric. All he wanted in that moment was darkness, cool air, and to be by himself.

He walked past Dougie and his friends (who paid absolutely no attention to him) like a boy in a dream, pushed through the door at the back of the gym, and walked out into the paved half-court. The cool fall air doused the fire in his cheeks, but not the euphoria. He looked up, saw a million stars, and understood that for each one of those million, there was another million behind it.

The universe is large, he thought. It contains multitudes. It also contains *me*, and in this moment I am wonderful. I have a right to be wonderful.

He moonwalked under the basketball hoop,

moving to the music inside (when he made his little confession to Ginny he could no longer remember what that music had been, but for the record it was the Steve Miller Band, "Jet Airliner"), and then twirled, his arms outstretched. As if to embrace everything.

There was pain in his right hand. Not big pain, just your basic ouch, but it was enough to bring him out of his joyous elevation of spirit and back to earth. He saw that the back of his hand was bleeding. While he was doing his whirling dervish bit under the stars, his outflung hand had struck the chainlink fence and a protruding jut of wire had cut him. It was a superficial wound, hardly enough to merit a Band-Aid. It left a scar, though. A tiny white crescent scar.

"Why would you lie about that?" Ginny asked. She was smiling as she picked up his hand and kissed the scar. "I could understand it if you'd gone on to tell me how you beat the big bully to a pulp, but you never said that."

No, he'd never said that, and he'd never had a bit of trouble with Dougie Wentworth. For one thing, he was a cheerful enough galoot. For another, Chuck

103

Krantz was a seventh-grade midget unworthy of notice.

Why *had* he told the lie, then, if not to cast himself as the hero of a fictional story? Because the scar was important for another reason. Because it was part of a story he couldn't tell, even though there was now an apartment building standing on the site of the Victorian house where he had done most of his growing up. The *haunted* Victorian house.

The scar meant more, so he had *made* it more. He just couldn't make it as much more as it really was. That made little sense, but as the glioblastoma continued its blitzkrieg, it was the best his disintegrating mind could manage. He had finally told her the truth of how the scar actually happened, and that would have to do.

10

Chuck's grandpa, his zaydee, died of a heart attack four years after the Fall Fling dance. It happened while Albie was climbing the steps of the public library to return a copy of *The Grapes of Wrath*—which, he said, was every bit as good as he remembered. Chuck was a junior in high school, singing in a band and dancing like Jagger during the instrumental breaks.

Grandpa left him everything. The estate, once quite large, had shrunk considerably over the years since Grandpa's early retirement, but there was still enough to pay for Chuck's college education. Later on, the sale of the Victorian paid for the house (small but in a good neighborhood, with a lovely back room for a nursery) he and Virginia moved into after their honeymoon in the Catskills. As a new hire at Midwest Trust—a humble teller—he never could have bought the place without Grandpa's inheritance.

Chuck flatly refused to move to Omaha to live with his mother's parents. "I love you guys," he said, "but this is where I grew up and where I want to stay until I go to college. I'm seventeen, not a baby."

So they, both long retired, came to him and stayed in the Victorian with him for the twenty months or so before Chuck went off to the University of Illinois.

They weren't able to be there for the funeral and burial, however. It happened fast, as Grandpa had

105

wanted, and his mom's folks had loose ends to tie up in Omaha. Chuck didn't really miss them. He was surrounded by friends and neighbors he knew much better than his mother's goy parents. A day before they were scheduled to arrive, Chuck finally opened a manila envelope that had been sitting on the table in the front hall. It was from the Ebert-Holloway Funeral Parlor. Inside were Albie Krantz's personal effects—at least those that had been in his pockets when he collapsed on the library steps.

Chuck dumped the envelope out on the table. There was a rattle of coins, a few Halls cough drops, a pocket knife, the new cell phone Grandpa had barely had a chance to use, and his wallet. Chuck picked up the wallet, smelled its old limp leather, kissed it, and cried a little. He was an orphant now for sure.

There was also Grandpa's keyring. Chuck slipped this over the index finger of his right hand (the one with the crescent-shaped scar) and climbed the short and shadowy flight of stairs to the cupola. This last time he did more than rattle the Yale padlock. After some searching, he found the right key and unlocked it. He left the lock hanging from the hasp and pushed the door open, wincing at the squeal of the old unoiled hinges, ready for anything.

11

But there was nothing. The room was empty.

It was small, circular, no more than fourteen feet in diameter, maybe less. On the far side was a single wide window, caked with the dirt of years. Although the day was sunny, the light it let in was bleary and diffuse. Standing on the threshold, Chuck put out a foot and toed the boards like a boy testing the water of a pond to see if it was cold. There was no creak, no give. He stepped in, ready to leap back the moment he felt the floor start to sag, but it was solid. He walked across to the window, leaving footprints in the thick fall of dust.

Grandpa had been lying about the rotted floor, but about the view he had been dead-on. It really wasn't much. Chuck could see the shopping center beyond the greenbelt, and beyond that, an Amtrak

107

train moving toward the city, pulling a stumptail of five passenger cars. At this time of day, with the morning commuter rush over, there would be few riders.

Chuck stood at the window until the train was gone, then followed his footprints back to the door. As he turned to close it, he saw a bed in the middle of the circular room. It was a hospital bed. There was a man in it. He appeared to be unconscious. There were no machines, but Chuck could hear one just the same, going *bip . . . bip . . . bip*. A heart monitor, maybe. There was a table beside the bed. On it were various lotions and a pair of black-framed glasses. The man's eyes were closed. One hand lay outside the coverlet, and Chuck observed the crescent-shaped scar on the back of it with no surprise.

In this room, Chuck's grandpa—his zaydee—had seen his wife lying dead, the loaves of bread she would pull off the shelves when she went down scattered all around her. It's the waiting, Chucky, he'd said. That's the hard part.

Now his own waiting would begin. How long would that wait be? How old was the man in the hospital bed?

Chuck started back into the cupola for a closer look, but the vision was gone. No man, no hospital bed, no table. There was one final faint *bip* from the unseen monitor, then that was gone, too. The man did not fade, as ghostly apparitions did in movies; he was just gone, insisting he had never been there in the first place.

He wasn't, Chuck thought. I will insist that he wasn't, and I will live my life until my life runs out. I am wonderful, I deserve to be wonderful, and I contain multitudes.

He closed the door and snapped the lock shut.

109

ABOUT THE AUTHOR

Stephen King is the author of more than sixty books, all of them worldwide bestsellers. His recent work includes *Never Flinch*, the short story collection *You Like It Darker* (a *New York Times Book Review* top ten horror book of 2024), *Holly* (a *New York Times* Notable Book of 2023), *Fairy Tale*, *Billy Summers*, *If It Bleeds*, *The Institute*, *Elevation*, *The Outsider*, *Sleeping Beauties* (cowritten with his son Owen King), and the Bill Hodges trilogy: *End of Watch*, *Finders Keepers*, and *Mr. Mercedes* (an Edgar Award winner for Best Novel and a television series streaming on Peacock). His novel *11/22/63* was named a top ten book of 2011 by the *New York Times Book Review* and won the Los Angeles Times Book Prize for Mystery/Thriller. His epic works *The Dark Tower*, *It*, *Pet Sematary*, *Doctor Sleep*, and *Firestarter* are the basis for major motion pictures, with *It* now the highest-grossing horror film of all time. He is the recipient of the 2020 Audio Publishers Association Lifetime Achievement Award, the 2018 PEN America Literary Service Award, the 2014 National Medal of Arts, and the 2003 National Book Foundation Medal for Distinguished Contribution to American Letters. He lives in Bangor, Maine, with his wife, novelist Tabitha King.

NEON Presents In Association with INTREPID PICTURES and RED ROOM PICTURES

in Association with QWGMIRE and FILMNATION ENTERTAINMENT

An INTREPID PICTURES and RED ROOM PICTURES Production A MIKE FLANAGAN Film "THE LIFE OF CHUCK"

TOM HIDDLESTON CHIWETEL EJIOFOR KAREN GILLAN MIA SARA CARL LUMBLY BENJAMIN PAJAK

with JACOB TREMBLAY and MARK HAMILL

Casting by ANNE MCCARTHY KELLIE ROY MORGAN ROBBINS

Music Supervisor JUSTINE VON WINTERFELDT Music by THE NEWTON BROTHERS

Costume Designer TERRY ANDERSON Editor MIKE FLANAGAN Production Designer STEVE ARNOLD

Director of Photography EBEN BOLTER, ASC, BSC Executive Producers MELINDA NISHIOKA D. SCOTT LUMPKIN

STEPHEN KING MOLLY C. QUINN MATTHEW M. WELTY ELAN GALE

Produced by TREVOR MACY, p.g.a. MIKE FLANAGAN, p.g.a.

Based on the Short Story by STEPHEN KING Written for the Screen and Directed by MIKE FLANAGAN

R | LANGUAGE

NEON   INTREPID PICTURES   FILMNATION entertainment   QWG MIRE   RTR RED ROOM